Why Are My Nuts _STILL_ in the Toilet Water?

Allen F. Mahon

SDC Publishing, LLC was established to promote and encourage aspiring writers and artists. It is a family oriented vehicle through which they can publish their work.

Contact SDC Publishing, LLC at allenfmahon@gmail.com

Or on the web at SDCPublishingLLC.com

This is a work of fiction. The events and characters described herein are imaginary and are not intended to refer to specific places or living persons (if there were any persons or places in this book). The opinions expressed in this manuscript are solely the opinions of the author and do not represent the opinions or thoughts of the publisher. The author has represented and warranted full ownership and/or legal right to publish all the materials in this book.

Other books by Allen F. Mahon

Embraced by Angels
Gone Home for Angels
The Siler Saga
Why are My Nuts in the Toilet Water
Soap Making Essentials
Ned's Journey
The Footlocker Book One: Discovery and Beginnings

DEDICATION

This book is dedicated to my bouts of writer's block. When I need a break from serious writing, this is where my mind wanders.

Allen F. Mahon

THIS BOOK IS PRINTED
IN LARGE PRINT FOR
ITS TARGET AUDIENCE.

FOR OBVIOUS REASONS.

Why Are My Nuts STILL in the Toilet Water?

Of course, Gravity. There is no escaping it. Also, I failed at inventing the "Nut Nest", If you remember from my previous book, I had great plans for the "Nut Nest". There was even a marketing plan.

Alas, I couldn't find a designer to design the thing. I did get some laughs. I tried to draw up the plans myself and I took them to a few potential manufacturers. Again… Laughs!

So… I built one myself from bits of Styrofoam and fishing line, 50 pound test, of course. During testing, my nuts were not the only things in the toilet water. At least it floated!

Being forever the optimist, I sent a model of the "Nut Nest" and an application to the United States Patent Office. I'm still waiting to hear back from them.

I still think it is a good idea. It just needs more research and development. I'll keep you posted as I make progress. I wouldn't want to leave you *hanging*.

Where is My Hair Going?

As I wrote about before, there are hairs growing in all the wrong places. Now I'm losing it! My hair, that is. Not in the places I don't want it, I'm losing it on my head.

One day, a couple of years back, my wife told me that my hair was receding. NAW!

I have always had a thick full head of luxurious hair. I was a blonde, blue eyed child. All the ladies wanted to pinch my cheeks because I was so cute.

By high school, my hair darkened a

little to a sandy blond, still a killer with the women, wink.

As I matured into a man, my hair settled into a brown color. It wasn't dark brown and it wasn't light brown. It was kind of a muskrat brown.

I cared for my hair lovingly. I shampooed, conditioned, dried it carefully and always had a comb in my pocket. I've never had dandruff nor head lice. Never a harsh chemical has ever ventured within 10 feet of my scalp. Well, there is that one time my barber talked me into getting a perm. We never spoke of it again.

Now its leaving me. After all we have been through together!

Thank God my beard is still thick and awesome! It gets more luxurious by the day. Of course it has turned gray. This fact elicits queries from small children, "Are you Santa?"

A Gastro-Intestinal ~~Upset~~ Update.

I'm back to eating whatever I want. The gas is still there but I no longer care. As long as you are quiet about it, you can release anywhere you wish. Also, if you put some air sanitizer in a small spritzer bottle that you can hide in your pocket, you are good to go. Automobiles and elevators could be an exception though.

As far as the little pine trees hanging on the ceiling fan in my office, I had to scrap that idea. My wife came into my office one day and turned the fan on high. The pine tree thingies were summarily chopped up and shot around the room like shrapnel. I thought it seemed like a good idea at the time.

My Body is Still Making all Those Strange Noises.

My body is still at it. Only now, it has added a few new noises. I started out with joint cracking. That was a solo act. Then it teamed up with a second noise to form a duo. Then a trio, then a quartet and so on until now, I am a full symphony.

My family says they don't hear it and maybe it is all in my head. Well let me tell you, I hear it loud and clear.

Wait! Now I hear ringing in my ears! GREAT!

Skin Tags.

I haven't had a skin tag since writing the previous book and I really don't want to talk about them.

Now, its Age Spots. I don't want to talk about those either.

I Have No Trouble With My Weight.

I still don't have a problem with my weight. My doctor, my wife, my daughters and pretty much everyone I know thinks I have a problem. So who are you going to believe? A couple hundred people or me?

If you watch the commercials for weight loss systems, they all promise the same thing. I'm a sixty seven year old man. Why would I want my body to look like a twenty something year old woman? Why would I want a twenty something year old woman's body. Oh… wait!

I'm Still Getting Smiles and Greetings From Women.

This has actually gotten better! Recently, a woman held the door for me and told me to go first. One young lady even asked if I needed her to carry a package for me. No, that one could have been a thief.

Anyhow, this is a very good reason to NOT lose weight. If I were to shed a pound or ten, would the smiles stop coming my way? My health be damned, it's not worth the risk!

I'm Not Getting Shorter.

I am still five feet eight inches tall. I suppose I can't really claim that statement. Since the incident three years ago, the nurse at my doctor's office doesn't bother measuring my height, she just takes my word for it.

At my next annual check-up, I will be six feet tall! Funny how that works.

Still Grunting When I Get Up.

Grunting has become one of the normal parts of my life. I don't hear it anymore so it doesn't bother me. It does bother my wife though.

We watch our youngest grandson during the week while my daughter works. My wife witnessed him grunting just like his Pop-Pop. For some reason she thinks I am setting a poor example. He's only three years old. If she thinks this is a poor example, she should ask the older two grandsons where they learned all of the things they do.

Why Does My Wife Not Hear 80% of What I Say Lately?

I've let this go. When I talk to all of my married male friends, they have the same problem. So… I've just let it go.

I No Longer Repeat Myself.

Because I've let it go!

Let's Talk Colonoscopy.

Let's get serious for a moment. This is both a touchy subject and an important one. This could save your life.

No one likes having a camera shoved up your butt. Well, maybe some of you do but I don't. At least they put me under.

What I didn't know at first was that they film up there. At least still photography. I know. I saw the eight by ten glossies. After the procedure the doctor came to talk to me and tell me what he found. I had a couple of polyps. He said that he removed them with no problem. I told him he could keep them because, so far, everything that has come out of there I've discarded.

He couldn't just tell me this, he had to pull out pictures like they were photos of his kids at a birthday party. "Look, here's Patty and Peter Polyp, the Polyp twins."

Really? Pictures? You went to medical school for God's sake! I believe you!

Of course, you know me, I had to look up butt polyps on the internet. It struck me that they look a lot like Skin Tags! No wonder I haven't had a skin tag for quite some time; THEY'RE GROWING IN MY ASS!

Afterthoughts

I know this book, like the previous one, didn't answer any questions because there were none posed. I hope it kept you entertained.

Age gracefully, my friends. Keep smiling and live life like you rented it.

ABOUT THE AUTHOR

Allen Mahon *still* lives and continues to age in Buchanan, Virginia with his wife, Randee, and his dog, Bailey (Charlie passed a while back). He is *still* retired from a career in the IT industry and *still* devotes most of his time writing (serious) novels and he is *still* pondering the workings of the Universe and of his body.

Made in the USA
Columbia, SC
16 December 2019